the invisible girl
in room thirteen

First published in e-book as The Girl in Room Thirteen on
1 December 2016

All rights reserved.

No part of this publication may be reproduced, stored in or introduced into a retrieval system, or transmitted, in any form or by any means (electronic, mechanical, photocopying, recording or otherwise), nor be otherwise circulated in any form of binding or cover other than that in which it is published without the prior written permission of the publisher.

Any person who does any unauthorized act in relation to this publication may be liable to criminal prosecution and civil claims for damages.

All characters, names, places, incidents, and dialogues are products of the author's imagination or are used fictitiously. Any resemblance to actual people, living or dead, events or locales is purely coincidental.

This is a work of fiction.

Independently published by Fiction for the Soul
www.stephensimpsonbooks.com

This edition is also available in

eBOOK

Have you checked behind you?

the invisible girl
in room thirteen

STEPHEN SIMPSON

1

I do not have a lot of memories from when I was little, but I do remember sitting in my back garden one rainy afternoon. It was starting to get dark, and I was starting to feel a little scared, but I was too afraid to go back into the house. The wind was cold, and it was giving me an earache, as it whipped around me. My tears had dried in streaks across my dirty cheeks and I puckered my lips to blow the hair hanging in front of me away from my face. Sniffing loudly, I twirled the daisy in my hand between my fingers. It spun and spun until the colours made a blurry white circle. I was captivated by the brilliant white petals and the buttery yellow middle. Taking one of the small white petals between two of my fingers carefully, I pulled it away from the heart of the flower, because the daisy would tell me if Mommy loved me or not. The petal pulled away from its centre effortlessly and I looked at it in wonder.

She loves me.

There were days when she smiled, and she laughed. She told me I was pretty, and she spun me around in her arms so that I could feel the wind on my cheeks. On those days we were happy, my Mommy and me. We would cuddle together, and she would watch my cartoons with me. I loved her smell then, she smelt warm. She made me feel safe and sheltered. I loved her more than anything else in the whole wide world, even more than Daddy.

She loves me not.

I was excited when I ran to her to show her my new dance, and to sing her the new song I made up all by myself. She yelled and told me to shut up, because I was giving her a headache. She ignored me when the tears started welling up in my eyes, but I quickly forced them to go away when she warned me, "Don't you dare start crying."

She loves me.

She still makes me dinner. Sometimes she still hugs me close and smiles widely when she sees me, making me feel all happy on the inside, making those warm feelings want to crawl back. She makes sure I have a bath every night and that I am wearing my warm jacket and hat when we must go out to the shops.

She loves me not.

By accident, I dropped my Sippy cup of milk onto the floor. The milk squirted out of the teat in a spray of milk against the wall. It ran down the wall in a tiny little waterfall and I could only stare at it. I cringed when she screamed so loudly, it hurt my ears, and she told me to, "Clean that up! Clean it now!"

She loves me.

When she thought I was asleep, she told me she was sorry. She was only tired, and she did not mean the horrible things she yelled at me. She did not mean it when she told me I was a selfish little brat. She did not mean it when she said that if I do not clean up my mess, she was going to kill me. She told me she would always love me, and I would always be her sunshine.

There was only one petal left and even though my little heart did not want to believe it, deep inside, I knew it to be the truth.

She loves me not.

2

As I grew older, I learned to never be a scared girl. I never worried about things which went bump in the night but standing in front of this door, I could feel an awareness I had not known before making a connection to things yet unknown.

Before my mum dropped me off here at boarding school and drove away again without a backwards glance, she tried to convince me why it would be good for me to come here. I pretended not to see she did not want to admit me being out of the way would be good for her and my stepfather.

She met my father here, but they did not really get to know each other until they met at a Christmas party at her parents' house approximately nine months before I was born.

Before my dad died and my mum married my stepfather, she used to tell me I was invincible, but if you replaced just two of the letters in that word it would be what I had become.

I was twelve when my mum remarried and that was

when I became invisible. Not invisible in a haunting the living from the grave kind of way, more like the unseen living kind.

Maybe she only wanted me to follow in her footsteps, to be educated in the proper English way, to rub shoulders with snobs and lower royalties. Maybe she thought I would find the love of my life like she did until he died. Maybe, always so many maybes.

This was only one of the reasons I was standing here with a Ouija board under my arm.

I shivered when I heard the wind howling around the corners of the old boarding house and my eyes darted nervously toward the door with the painted over numbers: 13

Rachel reached to take my hand, the bangles on her scarred wrist made a jangling noise. She had a wild mop of short, blonde, curly hair and a round face to match. Even though the shape of her face was round, the rest of her was really skinny so she looked a little top-heavy. "Don't be afraid, Alison," she said. "Even if Lily is still in there, it's not as if she can hurt you, you know."

Rachel and Sinéad took me under their wing when I arrived a week ago, but they were both a year older and I did not know if they were trustworthy as they were essentially part of the group who instigated this initiation, a dare I had no choice but to accept.

It was rumoured, Lily, the girl who used to reside in this room, fifteen years ago killed herself on the thirteenth of February, the day before Valentine's Day. Witnesses saw her walking into the mist shrouded lake behind the boarding house. They said, she killed herself because of a boy.

Rachel insisted, rubbing her wrist and making her bangles knock against each other like dull sounding Christmas bells, "If her ghost is in there, you can ask why she killed herself. Was it really just about a boy?"

Sinéad had the largest eyes I had ever seen. It was not ugly or humongous in a grotesque kind of way, it was breathtakingly beautiful. They were so green it looked eerie. Her long brown hair hung dead straight down past her shoulders and the tips brushed across her forearms. She said with an excited tone in her voice, "Last night, I read this magazine and in it, it says science has confirmed at the moment of death the body releases a sort of radiation. They called it an electromagnetic field. So… When somebody dies within a closed space, this force will imprint itself on the furniture and walls."

"I thought you said she drowned in the lake?" I said.

I did not know if I could go into a room which had been standing empty for over a decade and a half after someone had died in it, even if I needed to prove myself.

She ignored me. "That's why some people believe if somebody in the house died, all containers should be emptied of water because the water has been contaminated with the spirit of the dead person. It seems souls are attracted to water for some reason." Her eyes darted between Rachel and me, to see if we could confirm whether this was true or not.

If I was going to go into this room, I had to ignore her stories of ghosts and souls. "You cannot believe everything you read," I insisted.

Rachel asked, "Why then is this room always locked up? In all the years I've been here, no-one has ever stayed in it."

"What if there isn't even a ghost and the school board is just superstitious about the number thirteen?" I asked.

Rachel shrugged me off. "So, are you scared?"

"I wasn't when I accepted the dare, but now the two of you are talking about all these supernatural things and it's freaking me out."

Since I had accepted the challenge, I had been dreading the night of February the thirteenth.

Every time I walked past the fearsome door, I felt shivers scurry down my back. I could not avoid the door and had to walk by it several times a day by no choice of my own.

The boarding house was a two-storey building in the shape of a capital I. I lived on the first floor, five doors away from door number thirteen. Room number thirteen was the last room next to the large staircase which connected all the floors, so if I wanted to go anywhere I had to walk past that door which always felt like a black hole waiting to suck me into its depths if I lingered too long.

Rachel pulled a key from her pocket. "It's time," she announced and inched past me.

It was too late to wonder but I had to know. "How

come you have a key?"

"I've had this key for a while," she said with a shrug.

"But, why?"

Sinéad nudged me with her elbow and whispered, "Rachel has issues."

Rachel looked over her shoulder and gave Sinéad an annoyed look.

Sinéad winked. "Just kidding." She faced me and mouthed, "She really does."

Rachel sighed. "I'm just interested in all things paranormal, so one day I'd like to come here myself."

I said, hopeful, "You can take my place. Do the dare instead."

"I'm not ready yet," she said.

I felt insulted. She was not ready, but I was being forced to complete a dare just to prove I am worthy of being here at this boarding school, a place I did not even want to be in the first place.

She pushed the key into the lock.

I really did not want to do this.

Sinéad stood behind me and I felt a little claustrophobic standing between the two of them.

The only thought running repeatedly through my mind as I heard the key turn in the lock, was *I don't want to do this. I don't want to do this.*

The door swung open on stiff hinges which had not moved for a long time and made a soft moaning sound.

A gust ruffled the bangs from my forehead. The air smelled stale and musty, undisturbed for ages. I wondered where the sudden blast of wind had come from.

Sinéad shrieked softly and Rachel turned around to face her as she stepped aside. "Shh, do you want to wake the dead?"

They both giggled as if it was funny.

I don't want to do this. I don't want to do this. The words did not leave my lips.

Slowly I shuffled into the room, while they stayed on the other side of the threshold, being careful not to let their feet touch the boundary.

My breath frosted out of my mouth, just by stepping into the room and goose bumps erupted on my bare arms. The room was really cold, like walking out of a warm house on a cold winters' day. I shivered as I tried to fold my arms across my chest whilst still holding on to the Ouija board.

The light from the corridor shined into the room and only fell on the standard single bed, bedside table, chest of drawers and study desk. I could see the faded, daisy-printed curtains like the ones decorating my room hanging in front of the window. In the dim light, the paint on the walls was the identical shade of dark with age eggshell and the tiles on the floor were the same green as outside in the corridor.

The light did not reach the corners of the small, rectangular room and where the shadows remained it was dark, devoid of any colour and gloomy. It was not dark enough so someone or something could hide in them, but it still made me feel fearful. The shadows moved like they were breathing, and I quickly lifted my hand to rub my eyes.

Even though everything looked the same, it was not. The room had a different feel. It felt empty, cold and lonely.

3

Sinéad whispered behind me, "Okay. So, you know the rules. You have to stay here until after midnight." Her voice echoed in the room. The sound went on and on, further and further away, making the room sound bigger than it was.

Rachel pulled on Sinéad's arm and told her, "Close the door."

I pulled the Ouija board from under my arm and mumbled, "No way am I going to use this thing."

Rachel replied indignantly, "How do you think you are going to talk to her? Can you speak to the dead?"

"No, but I don't think I should be playing around with this stuff."

"Do you believe in ghosts, Alison?" She asked me.

"No."

"Well, then you'll be okay. They sell those things as board games, and only people who watch horror movies think they actually work, so just give it a try."

"Come," Sinéad said as she pulled Rachel away from the door. She had part of Rachel's shirt bunched in her fist and she leaned forward while still holding onto her. She reached the door handle with her fingertips and pulled it shut.

The only light remaining in the room was from the transom window above the door. Even though it was not bright, I could still see the shape of the bed, the bedside table and the study desk.

My eyes darted toward the cupboard doors to make sure they were closed, and my hand reached for the light switch next to the door without looking. After a few seconds, I found the protrusion on the wall and thumbed the switch down.

A quick glance around the room proved I was alone as I sat down on the floor, crossing my legs. With my back against the wall, so nothing could surprise me from behind, I pulled the board from its box and placed it on the floor in front of me. I touched the planchette with only my thumb and ring finger, lifting it and then putting it in the centre of the board. I did not really want it to touch me.

The dare required me to stay in room thirteen for the next three hours and to help me from being overwhelmed by a panic attack and failing to complete the dare, which was not an option, I pulled the thin sheet of rules from the box.

Even though the rules stated clearly: *Never use a Ouija Board alone!* I was alone in a normal room which felt not normal at all. I had a notion there was a presence in here with me. Even when my eyes searched every corner and saw nothing, I knew there was something watching me. I could feel it in the way my neck tingled and the way my skin erupted in goose bumps.

Never use a Ouija Board if you are depressed, stressed, irate, upset, bored, furious, sad, trepidatious, afraid, shocked, overconfident, or drowsy as you could let a demon into your life! My mum already allowed a demon into my life the day she married my stepfather. He was not abusive or threatening, and unlike in the movies he did not try to buy my love with things, he just pretended I did not exist and not long after they got married my mum stopped noticing me as well.

Her life was all about him and at fifteen I realized I wanted nothing as much as I wanted my mum's attention. I did not deny her any happiness in finding another husband, but I wanted her to sometimes put her needs and mine before what he always needed. I only wanted her to still be my mum, but she could not do both and be good at it. It had to be me or him, and she chose him.

Never use a Ouija Board if you think it is a game. As initiation at some boarding schools the older girls would raid rooms, pull mattresses off beds, make girls do the duck walk in a large circle, but not here. Here in these Gothic halls, something so mundane would be looked upon with disdain. A dare would be the only thing that would suffice.

I arrived late, so I missed the week of initiation when all the other new girls arrived. They all came through the ordeal okay, I tried to convince myself.

When Caitlyn, the head-girl, informed me, "The only way you'll ever be accepted here is if you accept the dare," I thought it was a joke. She shoved the Ouija board in my direction and added with a sneer, "Did you know, the very first Ouija boards were made from the wood of coffins. A coffin nail in the centre of the planchette window was used as the pointer."

A faint sound caught my attention, and I looked around the room. Seeing nothing, I decided it must have been the wind still howling and whistling around the corners of the boarding house and making the limbs of the large old trees outside creak while the leaves brushing against each other made sighing noises.

I looked down at the board. I had left the planchette in the middle of the board, not really caring where I put it, and now it had moved onto the word: Hello

Maybe, I shifted my leg without realising and knocked the planchette with my knee, I tried to rationalise why it had moved from the middle of the board and now the word, Hello, was magnified within the planchette window.

Besides, I thought I was supposed to be connected to the planchette, have my fingers resting on them gently so that unconsciously I would be answering my own questions.

I asked, even though I thought it was ridiculous, "Is anybody here?"

Nothing.

Then I took a sharp breath when I saw the planchette quiver on the board as I looked at it. I could not rationalize it away; pretend I had knocked it, or it was a draft or maybe even gravity. I saw it move.

Pushing away from the board, I felt my back push against the cold wall behind me. My palms pushed down on the green laminated tiles on each side of me to push me up from the floor so I could leave the room as quickly as my legs could move. I was so done with this. I did not have to prove my worth to anyone.

On legs that wanted to run but forgot how, I jumped over the board on the floor and when I landed, my right foot slipped on the tiled floor. It happened so quickly I did not have time to put my arms up to protect or to brace myself and I crashed headfirst into the door.

A sharp pain shot through my forehead and I could feel it ripple down my spine. Clutching my head in both my hands, I slid down the door and felt my T-shirt scrunch up against my back as it fought against the friction.

At first, I thought the hissing sound was from my T-shirt against the grain of the door, but when my eyes looked back at the board it was the noise the planchette was making as it moved across the letters. My eyes would not look away from the board as I watched the planchette spell the word: W.A.I.T.

I took a breath deep enough to lift my chest and closed my eyes for a second before I asked in a husky whisper, "What's your name?"

The planchette started moving all by itself to the L. Then it moved a little faster to the I, and even faster to the L. Y.

The roof light flickered on and off so fast it created a strobe light effect.

Leave. Now.

Then I remembered I wanted to be accepted, to be found worthy. I wanted someone to see me, not just notice me or be aware of me, I needed someone to really see me and I believed if I completed this dare I would deserve to be seen. After taking several deep breaths, I said, "My name is Alison."

The planchette spelt out the letters: I.K.N.O.W.

My breath hitched in my throat. As I read the letters, I also heard them spoken out loud in my head, drowning out my silent screams.

"Are you really dead?"

The planchette moved to the word: Yes.

Although I knew I was the only person in the room, my eyes still searched the empty corners. It could be that the senior girls were playing an initiation trick on me. Trying to scare me. Someone could be moving the planchette. Somehow. Or was I really talking to a ghost? The ghost of Lily?

"How did you die?" If I was really talking to the ghost of Lily, I would not get the known answer of walking into the lake and drowning. Lily would give me a reason.

My eyes followed the quick movements of the planchette on the board. B.R.O.K.E.N.

This time the word was only spelt. I did not hear it in my head.

"Why are you still here, Lily?" I asked, feeling sorry for

her. She must have been so sad and desperate at the time.

I felt a sudden savage force knock me back against the door so hard, the door rattled in its metal frame. A chilling gust of wind lifted my hair away from my face as a piercing voice inside my head yelled, *Because of you!*

I jumped to my feet so fast, I could not figure out how I got out of the room until I was standing outside in the corridor staring into the cold room. Shivers scampered through my body and made me feel weak. Everything that was keeping me together floated away from me and I fell onto my knees.

Sinéad and Rachel rushed to my side hurriedly and pulled me up from the floor.

"You were only in there for a second, we just closed the door," Sinéad complained. "You had to stay until after midnight."

"I was in there for hours." I looked at them confused. "Whatever. I don't care. I'm not going in there again no matter what you say or do." My outburst shocked even me. Before I became invisible, I was never timid. However, sly and cunning looks meant to demean without saying a word had the power of stripping confidence and assurance. Being in room thirteen had given me the courage to stand my ground, or at least try to be more assertive. My mum might have brought me here for her own selfish reasons, and at the time I felt a deep and utter sadness. I now came to realise, coming here was the best thing that could have ever happened to me.

Sinéad huffed, "Fine. We're only trying to help."

I turned away from them to walk to my room. "I don't need your help."

Sinéad asked, "What's wrong with you?"

Rachel said, "Leave her, she's kinda weird."

Ignoring them, I pushed open my bedroom door and after I walked into the room, the door swung closed behind me without me touching it. The wind rushing past me sounded like an exhaled breath.

At my cupboard, I pulled open the doors and reached for my towel when a scraping noise behind me made me glance over my shoulder. Nothing was out of place, so I turned back and pulled my nightgown from a hanger. I was determined not to let my experience in room thirteen make me feel anxious or afraid. I was happy to be out of that room, but I felt different. Somehow, I felt stronger, invincible like my mum always used to say I was.

From the corner of my eye, I saw a dark shadow shift across the mirror on the inside of the cupboard door. I turned to face the mirror and felt threatened by the expression in my own eyes as they stared back at me. It was there only for a second and then my own brown eyes were looking back at me.

A loud noise made me spin around completely. Utterly terrified, my panicked eyes scanned the room. My lips trembled, about to ask who was there when I was brutally shoved into the cupboard and fell back into my hanging clothes.

4

I woke up in my cupboard, not really knowing why I was laying in a bundle on the floor with half of my clothes on top of me. Then, memories flooded back, and I remembered every horrific second of the night before.

The whole morning, I was trying to shake the feeling of dread and even if it was all I could think about, I wanted to pretend it did not happen.

I only arrived here a week ago and I really did not want everyone to think I was mad in the head. It was better they first got to know me. I had to make a good first impression. Find my place in the world where I was not invisible.

When most of us die our souls move on, but some souls remain in a place of anger and revenge, a lot closer to this world and when I entered room thirteen I opened a door to this other side and I did not know how to close it again.

It was the third period, Technology when I walked into the classroom and sat down beside Evelyn.

For a moment we sat listening to the sounds of feet rushing through the halls outside the classroom and locker doors being slammed shut.

Evelyn turned to me with a curious look in her big blue eyes. "Did last night go well? Any ghosts?" She flicked her shoulder length blonde hair hanging on the one side of her head to the other.

"I don't ever want to talk about it," I dismissed her. If I did not talk about it out loud then I could pretend the curious and unusual feelings I had since being in room thirteen was just my imagination. Feelings which were trying to overwhelm me.

After I left room thirteen last night, I stood up for myself for probably the first time in my life ever.

Before, I was timid and did what I was told without question because I wanted the approval of those around me.

Now, it felt as if I was warring against an inner demon.

The school bell rang, and the other students started filtering into the classroom.

Evelyn cleared her throat. "So, you looking forward to the dance tonight?"

"No, not really. You?" I looked up from scrolling through my phone to make eye contact with her.

"I have multiple options for a date, would you like to go in a group with us?"

"I don't have to tag along."

Evelyn added, "Yeah, but showing up at a party alone would look rather pathetic and I do have a partner situation. It would be easier for me to text them and tell them we're all going in a group. I'm not very good at decision making."

I felt a strange twist in the pit of my stomach and the simmering feeling of rage tried to overwhelm me. I had to really push hard to make the feeling fade as I convinced myself it would be nice not to arrive on my own.

Just then Mrs Peterson walked into the classroom and started handing out sheets of paper.

The girl closest to the door complained, "But Miss, we have the Valentine's Dance tonight."

The girl sitting behind her agreed after she picked up the sheet of paper from her table to scan it, "It's not fair, Miss."

"Okay, girls, settle down. You have a week to complete the assessment and I only want your best efforts," Mrs Peterson explained. "You can start now."

I read through the instructions and started working on it straight away.

Twenty minutes later, Evelyn nudged me and whispered, "Okay, it's all arranged. We'll meet at seven in front of the main entrance to the school."

I whispered back, leaning closer to her, "What if I get there before you?"

She scrolled through the photos on her phone until she landed on an image of two good looking boys. "These are Colin and Oliver." She pointed her finger at each one as she said their names. "So, if I'm not there yet just introduce yourself and wait with them."

As if.

My eyes lingered on Oliver, who had a tanned complexion with a smattering of freckles on the crest of his cheeks. His dark hair was swept back from his forehead, but it was his eyes and his smile which caught my attention. His eyes were a shade of blue. Sometimes blue eyes just looked washed out, but his eyes were radiant. His smile, even though just pixels on a screen made me want to smile as well. I think I might have fallen in love with him just then.

"So, you're game?" Evelyn looked at me for confirmation.

"Yeah," I agreed. She was right. It would look pathetic if I arrived at a dance dedicated solely to the idea of love, alone.

The bell rang and she grabbed her bag. "So, I'll see you tonight. Seven. Front entrance."

I watched her rush through the door before any of the other girls even got up from their chairs.

We were allowed to take the rest of the day off to get ready for the Valentine's Dance, and when I got to my dorm room, I started doing all the little things needed to prepare for a dance. Things I had no intention of doing this morning, but four hours later and things had changed. I liked Oliver. Well, I liked the look of Oliver. He might turn out to be completely not my type, but I wanted to try to look my best. To impress.

At fifteen minutes to seven, my nails were done, my make-up applied with the help of a few YouTube tutorial videos and my black hair, which I had in curlers since two o'clock this afternoon already started to lose their curl.

Standing in front of the mirror in my room, I pulled up the zip of the black, fitted dress I was wearing. The only decent dress I had brought with me was the same black dress I wore to my father's funeral. When he died a part of me died as well. There was a hole in my heart which would never go away. Depressing, I know, wearing it to a dance of love, but it was either jeans or this.

Taking a deep breath, I swung the cupboard door shut. A gust of air pushed the door open again and I quickly dared a glance at the darkness within. Forcefully I pushed against the door until I heard the little latch at the top of the door catch.

I grabbed my handbag from the dressing table and just as I reached my door, I heard a faint creak. Looking over at my cupboard, the door was open again.

Pulling my dorm door open, I saw girls streaming down the hallway, dressed in shades of red. I joined them and followed them down the stairway, before heading for the entrance doors of the main school building.

"Alison," Evelyn called as soon as I rounded the last corner. I walked over to her where she was standing to the side with Oliver and Colin.

I was never a romantic, maybe a dreamer but never a romanticist. Sometimes I dreamt there was a balance between good and bad, and here it was. The bad of my dad dying, my invisible state, being abandoned at boarding school was suddenly perfectly balanced by the boy in front of me.

After quick introductions, Evelyn grabbed Colin's hand and pulled him down the hall with her, leaving me to follow with Oliver who fell into step next to me.

When we reached the entrance doors to the assembly hall, he tilted his head a little, gestured with his hand for me to walk ahead of him and smiled an amused, crooked smile.

Self-consciously, I stepped ahead and walked into the hall, which had been transformed into a red and white monstrosity with long, sheer, see-through curtains hanging from the high vaulted ceilings like banners in old, medieval castles. A gentle, fragrant breeze blew from hidden vents and made the material sway, and together with the soft lighting created a mystical illusion.

I had to walk past Sinéad and Rachel, who waved in greeting. Rachel gave me a big smile and said, "You look gorgeous, Alison. You clean up nicely."

The earth did not open and swallow me whole.

Oliver reached for my hand and held onto it as he steered me through the crowd of people and tables to get to Evelyn and Colin on the other side of the room.

I tried to pull my hand out of his, but he held my fingers a little tighter.

A song started playing and students started moving toward the dance floor, making it even more difficult for us to navigate our way to Evelyn and Colin.

Abruptly, Oliver changed direction and started pulling me toward the dance floor instead.

"What are you doing?" I asked.

"If you can't beat them, join them," he said with a nonchalant shrug.

On the dance floor, he turned suddenly to face me, and I walked into him. My hands coming up to stop me from crashing into him, landed on his chest.

He smiled as he looked down at me, before folding his arm around my waist and pulling me closer. "I never thought of this as a slow song, but if you insist."

Again, the earth refused to open and swallow me whole. My heart was beating wildly in my chest. If I was a cartoon drawing, my heart would be going kaboom, kaboom on a string attached to me.

He said, "In case you got confused with the introductions, I'm the one called Oliver."

"And I'm Alison, in case you missed it too."

"No, I got it. Thanks for agreeing to be my date, though, last minute and all."

"Wait..."

"What? You didn't and I basically kidnapped you?" He chuckled.

"No. But... Evelyn said you both asked her, and she couldn't choose." I really hoped I did not just share a secret Evelyn did not want to be shared.

"They've been dating for two years, and if I made a play for her, Colin would maim me, so, it seems she told you a tall tale. Sad someone had to lie to get me a date, don't you think?"

I wondered why, though. Surely, he could get any girl he

set his sights on.

"Not going to say anything?" He asked after a few moments of awkward silence.

I raised my eyebrows as I looked up at him and smiled a little. "Not really. I think you're the one telling tall tales."

"Wow! You've finally found a girl who's even better looking than you," a stocky boy said, looking over his shoulder while gyrating his hips.

Oliver let out a booming laugh.

The girl dancing with the stocky boy, Violet, agreed, "I've seen a thousand girls look at him like you are right now."

Earth. Open. Swallow.

Violet danced around the stocky boy so that she could lean into me, and said close to my ear, "And this is the first time I've ever seen him look back at a girl like he's looking at you."

My heart reacted with a jolt.

"Violet," he growled and turned us away from the two chatty dancers.

I dared a glance up at him and saw a faint rose-colour taint the crest of his cheeks. Was he blushing?

5

I felt possessed.

Dark and soft lights flashed in the room, the throbbing pulse of the music, the movement of dancing bodies, his arms around my waist, everything around me culminated in making me feel alive and I had not felt alive in a long time. I had been unseen for even longer.

"Alison," Oliver said, pulling me back from my thoughts. "I hope that jerk, Evan, didn't make you feel awkward."

I looked up at him, and into his clear blue eyes. "I know he was just joking. How gullible do you think I am?"

"He likes to mess with me, is all," he explained. "Are you looking forward to going camping next weekend?"

"What camping? It's the first I'm hearing of it."

"That's when the fun really starts around here." His eyes sparkled as a mischievous grin pulled on the corners of his mouth.

"Both schools? Boys & girls?" I could not see how boarding school could ever get to be fun. It was supposed to be a form of punishment, wasn't it?

He answered with a wink, "Separate tents, though."

The music changed, and I started to pull away from him, but he pulled me even closer. Good thing we were in the middle of the dance floor with about a hundred bodies surrounding us. We could not be seen too clearly by the chaperones who made sure we all kept respectable distances from each other, just in case the mere touch of our bodies would lead to impregnation.

"I hear you went into room thirteen and survived to tell the story," he said jokingly.

I shook my head, and at the same time, I felt a sharp pain in the nape of my neck, like a precursor to a headache.

The suppressed feeling of rage I have had since leaving room thirteen tried to overwhelm me, and I pushed away from him. "I need to powder my nose."

"No worries," Oliver said as he took my hand and led me through the dancers between us and the door.

"I know the way," I told his back.

When we entered the well-lit corridor, he slowed down until I was beside him. "I know you know the way. I just needed a breath of air as well. Too many people in the same room make me feel claustrophobic sometimes."

The designated toilets were just across the hallway, but there was a long queue.

With my hand still in his, he pulled me past the line of girls. Leaning down, with his lips brushing my ear, he whispered, "I know of another one where there'll be no waiting."

"How…" I started asking, but then realised this was not his first dance here and I am not the first girl he had walked down this corridor. The simmering ember of rage in the pit of my stomach was ignited by this thought and it glowed red hot. The feeling threatened to burst from me.

Since my mum married again, I had grown good at hiding my feelings. Hide the hurt, the anger, the rejection and the pain. I always had my emotions under control, always, until now. Was it because here I did not have to hide them as well as I did at home?

"So, Lily?" He turned to look at me.

"Yeah?" Then I realised he had called me Lily, and I answered as if I was her. I know now I should never have gone into that room. The rules warned me, deep down I knew I should not mess with supernatural things, but I did it anyway to prove I am worthy, to get the approval of people who still did not see me. I looked at him with a frown and asked unsure, "Lily?"

"You know. The girl from room thirteen," he explained.

"What about her?"

"Do you think she really killed herself?"

"Probably. There were witnesses," I said dismissively. The only thing everyone wanted to talk about was the sudden demise of Lily, fifteen years ago. I did not want to be reminded. Since being in room thirteen and meeting Lily, I felt as if we had a connection. We were one.

"I wonder who the mystery guy she was in love with was," I said.

"Do you think he knew she walked into the lake and drowned herself because of him? Rumours say he married some stuck-up, rich girl. Did you know he dumped her the day she killed herself, the day before Valentine's Day?"

"I've heard all the rumours, but do you know who the guy was?"

"I think it was some guy called, Rob or Robin or Robert, something like that anyway. You can look it up in the School Journals in the library, though. I'm sure they have them all there."

An irrational impulse pushed me to know who the boy was who broke Lily's heart. I had to see his face. "I'd like to find out who he was," I said. "I think it'd be interesting to know."

"I'll help you if you wanted me to." The crest of his cheeks shaded a colour of pink again. He certainly was adorable. The one moment I knew I could really love Oliver and the very next second I felt inexplicable anger. I could not understand where the feeling I had to avoid him at all cost was coming from. I felt an acute awareness that he would have no trouble breaking my heart and he was not to be trusted. No boy was ever to be trusted.

He asked, "Tomorrow? We could start early."

"How early is your early?" I asked.

"The library opens at ten on a Saturday, too early for you?"

We had reached the bathroom, and I pushed the door open, telling him across my shoulder, "You know it's kind of embarrassing having you wait here for me. Maybe we could meet back at the drinks table?"

He nodded and I watched him walk away before I let the heavy door swing shut behind me.

The bright fluorescent lights glared in the mirrors to my side and as I pushed lightly on one of the slightly open cubicle doors, I saw a shadow move across the mirror and there was a flash of silver, maybe a reflection off the tap.

At first, I only saw her wide eyes where she was sitting on the toilet seat, then the gaping hole in her stomach which was a mass of blood and ripped flesh. Her insides lay on the ground between her feet. On the cubicle wall, written with a finger in oozing blood no doubt from Shannon's body, was: $1 + 1 = 3$

A scream erupted from the bottom of my soul as I collapsed on the floor.

The bathroom door burst open, the doorknob banging on the wall behind it.

"Alison?" Oliver asked in a panicked voice as he rushed toward me. "What's going on? Are you okay? I heard screaming."

He glanced into the stall and the colour drained from his face. His eyes were big, full of the look of horror as he pulled me up from the floor and pushed me out of the room.

Holding me close to him, he dialled the police. "Someone's dead… Here in the girls' toilet." He listened for a while, before he said, "Yes. At the school dance." He ended the call and after he pushed his phone back into his pocket, his arms tightened around me, pulling my head closer to his chest. "Shh, Alison. It's okay," he whispered. "The police are on their way."

My body shook in his arms.

"What happened?" He asked.

My teeth chattered as I tried to say, "All that blood."

"Do you know her?"

"I think her name is… was Shannon something. We're… were in the same English class."

"Did you see who did it?"

"No. I didn't see anyone else. Did you see someone in the hallway?" I tried to move my head to look up at him, but he held me steady against his chest.

The sound of footsteps was running toward us, and I tried to pull away from Oliver even harder. I had to get away from here, as fast as possible.

"It's just the security guard," he reassured me. "Look."

I opened my eyes and saw a pot-bellied man in a khaki brown shirt approaching. When he reached us, he was breathing hard as he hitched his trousers up around his stomach. His eyes darted around as he said, "Got a call from the police, they're on their way. Someone got killed, they said, and I must secure the crime scene."

Oliver told him, "In there." Pointing to the door of the bathroom.

He stepped back and stood in the door, folding his arms across his chest so that they were resting on his belly and faced us. There was a serious look on his face.

We stood in silence for the most part of twenty minutes when there was a commotion at the top of the hallway and a whole group of people were streaming toward us.

I recognised the principal, one or two teachers and at least three police officers.

The security guard said, "In here, Constable Fraser."

Constable Fraser motioned with his hand for the other two police officers to join him and they entered the bathroom cautiously.

When Constable Fraser stepped out of the room again, his face was insipidly pale, and he wiped beads of sweat from his face.

As he stepped toward Oliver and me, the other two police officers ushered the principal and the teachers back up the hall. I tried to hear what they were saying but they were all talking at the same time.

"Who discovered the body?" Constable Fraser asked, looking from me to Oliver.

"I did," I said as I stepped away from Oliver and he let me go.

Constable Fraser pulled a notebook and a pen from his top shirt pocket. He flipped it open to a blank page and squinted up at me, while his head was still bent down. "Name?"

"Alison Locke."

He lifted his head and looked at me, taking in my features. "Not a very common surname around here. Are you family of Roger Locke who went to school here about fifteen years ago?"

I looked at him confused. "He's my dad."

For a long moment, he just looked at me without saying

anything, then wrote something in his notebook before asking, "How is your dad?"

"Did you know him?"

"I did. We went to school together. I just have a few questions, then you can go."

6

A police officer started taping crime scene tape around the door to the bathroom and flashes of light erupted from the interior every now and again as someone was taking photos of what was left of Shannon.

Oliver held his arm around my waist as he steered me back to the hall where all the lights were switched on, turning the once mystical, romantic atmosphere in a stark, austere reality of polished wood floors and white walls.

Everyone in the room was standing in groups talking in hushed, panicked voices. Police officers were standing by the doors to make sure no-one left until everyone was questioned.

Oliver led me to the table where Evelyn and Colin sat with Violet and Evan.

When we reached them, Evan jumped up and asked with a hint of fear in his voice, "They say she was gutted?"

I flinched.

Oliver said, "Thanks, Evan."

Evelyn wiped tears from her cheeks. "Who could have done such an awful thing?"

Colin draped his arm across her shoulders to comfort her. "They say it couldn't have been a girl who'd done it."

Evan added, "Yeah, I heard Shannon was completely hollowed out. It takes a man to do something like that." He looked at Oliver. "Hey, didn't you used to date Shannon?"

I took a step away from Oliver, as he said, "I wouldn't say we dated."

Colin chuckled.

Evelyn asked, "Did you tell the police you dated?"

Oliver looked at her offended. "Are you suggesting I'm the one who killed her? Alison was with me the whole time."

Just then a voice boomed in the hall, "Girls. Go straight to your rooms. Boys, to the bus. No loitering."

Oliver turned to face me. "Are we still meeting at the library tomorrow?"

I nodded my head.

"Ten?" He asked.

"Yeah," I said as I pushed past him. I could not stop wondering why Constable Fraser looked at me with recognition in his eyes, and then the strange way he looked at me after he learned my dad was Roger Locke.

Principal Jackson walked up behind me and pulled me into her scrawny frame. She was very tall and very skinny, sometimes she reminded me of a crow. Her usually neatly set black hair was dishevelled and her dark suit looked crumpled. "Are you okay, Alison?" She asked. "Such a horrible thing to happen. Don't worry, the police will find who did it. You don't have to be afraid. The police will be here all night and we got some extra security, so whoever did it won't be able to harm you or any of the girls tonight."

I felt uncomfortable standing so close to her, so I squirmed out of her embrace. "I'm okay. Really."

"I've called Dr Smithers. He'll be here any minute."

I assured her, "I am really okay, though."

How could I tell her or anyone there was a part of me that believed Shannon deserved to die? Although I did not see it with my own eyes, I knew she was trying to get Oliver's attention since we walked into the hall together.

"Do you want me to get one of the girls to walk with you to your room?" She asked as her eyes scanned the room.

I just wanted to be alone. "It's okay. Thank you, Ms Jackson."

She gave me a worried look as I moved away from her.

I walked through the hall and through the corridors back to the boarding house. When I stepped to the top of the stairs and turned the corner with room thirteen right beside me, I could have sworn I saw a light from beneath the door. It was there for just a second, just from the corner of my eye, easily imagined. An eerie feeling almost overwhelmed me, but then Rachel called my name and I turned to look at her.

"Are you okay?" Rachel asked from the stairs, her foot resting on the first step which would take her up to the second floor.

I nodded my head and gave her a grim smile. Without saying a word, I turned away from her and continued walking down the passage to my own room.

The eerie feeling followed me even after I closed my room door and looked around the small space. Everything looked the same as when I left earlier tonight to go to the Valentine's dance.

The light in the room dimmed suddenly, but the room did not go dark. There was a strange scratching sound coming from under my bed.

Slowly, I stepped closer to the single bed pushed against the wall and knelt next to it, pulling at a corner of the duvet to lift it.

With my head almost touching the ground I peered in under the bed but there was nothing besides darkness.

"What are you doing?"

I twisted around fast and looked up at Sinéad standing by my room door.

She was looking down at me with a deep frown. "Are you okay?"

Pushing myself up off the floor, I wiped my hands on my knees. "Yeah," I said, distracted.

"You're acting different since you went into room thirteen last night," she said as she walked into my room and sat down on the edge of my bed, not waiting for an invitation.

"I just have a lot on my mind, that's all," I apologised as I leaned against my desk. Absent-mindedly I traced my fingers over the bevelled letters of the Ouija board I had left there last night.

She watched my fingers for a while. "Did anything strange happen in that room?"

I picked up the planchette and held it in my hands as I looked back at her, making eye contact. "No. Nothing."

"I'm worried about you and I don't think you should be alone after finding Shannon's body."

"It's funny, seeing her cut open like that from her throat all the way down to her navel. It doesn't feel real. It feels like something from a movie or I just imagined it." Placing the planchette on the board, I crossed the small space between the desk and the bed to sit down next to her. "Do you know anything at all about the girl in room thirteen? Do you know anything about Lily?"

She shook her head.

I looked at her. "You remember what you told me last night?"

She looked at me confused.

"That thing about electro-something energy. The energy we're supposed to leave behind when we die."

Understanding dawned on her face. "I believe it's true. We're all made of energy, aren't we? So, when we die, that energy needs to go somewhere."

I pondered her words for a while, looking at the Ouija board on my desk. "I guess you're right."

Sinéad started to stand up. "So, if you're sure you're okay, I better get going. I have a new roommate now. Amber. You should come around to my room sometime and meet her. She's nice." She shrugged her shoulders. "So far, that is."

"Thanks for coming to check if I'm okay," I said as I walked with her to the door.

"No worries." She smiled. "If you're scared or anything, you know where I am."

I watched her walk away until she rounded the corner at the end of the long corridor with its shiny floor and dull lighting.

In my room behind me, something made a scratching noise.

I quickly looked over my shoulder and the sound stopped immediately.

Stepping into my room, my eyes darted to the Ouija board first and I saw the planchette had moved. It was now pointing at 'Hello'.

I felt disconnected from finding Shannon dead and gutted in the toilet. Everybody kept asking if I was okay, but I was perfectly fine. Not a bother. I probably should be suffering from shock.

Determined, I closed my bedroom door and went to bed.

7

Standing on the lawn in front of the Library, I looked up at the building framed in stark contrast to the grey, oppressive clouds in the background and I understood my life would never be the same again. I had never thought a lot about destiny, but maybe this was mine. Maybe it was my destiny to find out what happened to Lily.

Tall, green-leaved trees basking in the weak light of the sun, stood on both sides of the square building.

The surrounding colours seemed to drain from the world as I headed up a couple of stairs and pushed past the frosted glass doors.

I stood in the door for a moment, trying to see if Oliver was here already while a fan blew warm air on to me from a vent just above the door frame.

Bookshelves lined every wall of the large room, and some shelves were placed in a labyrinth of aisles at the back of the room. A row of shelves in the front boxed in an area with five large wooden tables and soft lights.

Oliver waved me over from a table at the back.

As I reached him, he smiled and said, "Morning. Are

you okay after last night… You know..."

I did not want to be reminded of the bloody remains that used to be Shannon. "It's so quiet in here. A little eerie," I said looking around the room as I shrugged out of my jacket.

He looked around the sombre room. We were the only two people here, besides the librarian who was standing behind the high, wooden reception desk at the front of the large room, checking books back in.

"There's hardly ever anyone here, except when it's exams," Oliver explained. He said, again, "Last night..."

"I don't want to talk about it, Oliver." My voice sounded too harsh in the hushed atmosphere.

He recoiled, holding his hands up, palms facing me. "Okay. Not a word."

I sat down beside him, looking at the yearbooks he already had stashed on the table.

"I've been here a while already." He looked bashful. "I couldn't sleep so I thought I'd get a head start and gather all the yearbooks so long."

I began digging through the pile of books, looking for the last year my mum went to school here.

When I found the one, I was looking for, I flipped through the pages until I landed on the individual photographs and quickly found my mother's young face beaming up at me. Poking at her name in bold font below the black and white image: Dianne Cameron, I said to Oliver, "This is my mum when she went to school here. Her last year."

Oliver moved his chair closer and his shoulder pushed against mine as we both looked down at the image. "You look a lot like her."

I rolled my eyes without looking away from her youthful face. "I suppose."

"What did Lily look like?" He asked and tried to pull the book away from me.

I put my palm on the book to keep it where it was. "I'll look," I insisted as I turned the page and scanned the names printed below each photo. Two pages later, there was a memorial page with the name Lily Martin in large, bold font under a photo which took up most of the white space on the page. I said softly, "She died before photo day."

In the photo, Lily was smiling. She was very pretty, and I could not help noticing she was much prettier than my mum. Her symmetrical face was framed with blonde hair, cut in a short style, but she had a feminine grace about her so even if her hair was all shaved off, she would still be beautiful. Looking at the image of Lily made me feel a deep sense of loss, sadness and regret.

"Do you think if Lily could do it all over again, to change the way she ended her life, do you think she would think twice before doing something so drastic?"

He did not answer my question as we both stared at the image for a while as if we were having a minute of silence for her.

Oliver said, "It's not an official school photo, look there's a hand on her shoulder."

I leaned down to have a closer look. The person who was standing next to Lily on the photo was cropped out, but fifteen years ago I guess nobody thought about Photoshop to erase the hand on her shoulder.

"There's a class ring or something on that finger," I said poking at the image.

Oliver leaned even closer, our heads and our shoulders were now pushed together.

He leaned down even more. His nose was almost touching the paper. "It looks similar to the ring our head boy wears."

I shoved him with my shoulder to get him to move. "Let me see." It did look like the rings they gave head boys. I knew because my dad had one. "Who was the head boy that year at your school," I asked even though I already knew the answer.

He shrugged his shoulders as he looked at me.

"It was my dad. Roger Locke," I said softly.

He looked shocked. "Say again. You're saying the guy who broke Lily's heart was your dad?"

Unable to form words I could only nod my head.

"So..." He started. "Your dad and Lily..."

"Yes. It seems my mum stole my dad from Lily." I looked up at him, not sure if I should tell him the sordid history of how I came about. Taking a deep breath, I said, "I've always known my mum fell pregnant with me while she was still at school. You see, I was born in September, fifteen years ago. By the time it was Valentine's Day that year my mum was already a few weeks pregnant with me.

They must have just found out and he must have told Lily or maybe even my mum told Lily, we would probably never know how it happened exactly, so basically, my dad cheated on Lily and ultimately my parents drove Lily into the lake that night."

I wiped my face with my hands and filled my lungs with air. "I didn't know. I didn't know my dad was in a relationship with someone else. They always made it sound so romantic and told me even though they always knew about each other, going to segregated classrooms yet part of the same school, they only really met at a Christmas party at my mum's house. They spend every second of the Christmas break together and the story of how they fell in love always seemed so perfect, so idyllic. Obviously, I was gutted to learn I was not a planned baby, only an accident, but I got over it because how many children are really planned these days?"

I looked at him for confirmation, but his eyes were focussed on the image of Lily smiling happily at the lens of the camera.

I continued in a soft whisper, "Sad thing is, I knew my dad went out with another girl before my parents started their relationship, but truth be told, it never bothered me. It's part of life sometimes, isn't it?" My stomach twisted in anguish and as a feeling of rage threatened to overwhelm me, I felt a headache starting to grow.

"Before your parents met at the Christmas party, they probably never spoke to each other and when they did, they most likely realised how much they had in common and grew to love each other. It happens."

Am I really the reason Lily was broken? Why she walked into the lake that night? When I was in room thirteen and I asked her why she was still here, she shoved me and said it was all because of me. Now I understood what she meant. If not for me, my dad most probably would not have ended their relationship. Lily would not still be here, haunting room thirteen, waiting for someone to see her. Even though she saw everything, nobody ever saw her. Just like me, she was invisible.

A voice inside my head said, *together we could be invincible.*

8

As we walked down the stairs away from the library, Oliver asked, "Are you going to phone and ask your mum?"

I shrugged. "They're on a retreat somewhere. No phones allowed."

As we approached the large, imposing building, I looked up at all the neatly spaced, square windows and my eye caught the little gargoyles on top of the roof looking down at the garden in front of the building. The pathway to the doors had a neatly trimmed hedge on both sides.

He walked with me to the front door. "We could've gone into the city to watch a movie maybe or go have a bite to eat that doesn't resemble mass production, but I have a rugby match this afternoon." He gave me a hopeful look.

It sounded like an invitation, but I said, "I'm a little tired, but maybe I'll see you there." I smiled and nudged his shoulder. "See if you have any talent or if you're just wasting your time."

He chuckled and pushed his hands into his jean's

pockets.

I took a step closer to the door. "So, I'll see you later?"

He nodded his head, turned around and walked away.

I walked up to my room and then lay down on my bed. I was not sure if I fell asleep but after laying on my bed staring up at the ceiling for a really long time, images started playing on the matte white paint above me.

Lily's large eyes looked haunting in the centre of soft pink eyeshadow and up close, her white skin seemed to give off its own luminescent glow. Her blonde hair was ruffled by the wind blowing over the surface of the lake. She was wearing a long, white, old-fashioned night gown and the light from the full moon silhouetted her legs through the material which hung to her ankles.

The mist on the lake swirled toward her as she walked closer to the water and the large grey boarding house loomed behind her, while the gargoyles on the roof seemed to be focused on her movements.

At the edge of the lake, where the wind was making small ripples on the surface of the water, creating tiny waves, she stopped for a moment.

She started pacing and ranting, "I guess he just didn't love me enough. One and one makes three."

Then, the mist embraced her and welcomed her to a refuge of lost souls. It coaxed her to take another step and then another. I watched her walk into the water until she disappeared in the mist.

The image faded and I stretched lazily.

Sunlight was filtering through my window and the sky

was a deep azure blue.

The earlier grey clouds from this morning had all rushed away to go and spread their dreariness somewhere else.

Deciding fresh air and being social would probably do me good, I got ready to go to Oliver's game. I was sure most of the girls were already there and that was why the boarding house was so quiet.

To the side of the boarding house, there was a clump of trees and I decided to take a shortcut through the little forest to the other side where the boy's school's sports fields started.

It was so quiet I could hear the birds tweeting in the treetops and far-off I could hear a crowd cheering. I hoped it was Oliver who scored a try.

I walked a little faster to get there quicker and then I heard a sob. My head spun in that direction, and I recognised Belinda, who stayed in the room opposite me. Instead of walking on and ignoring them, something compelled me to duck behind a tree and to watch them.

Barry was leaning against a tree trunk, with his hands in his pockets, while Belinda was standing in front of him.

Belinda pouted. "You said you loved me."

The boy smiled. "I meant it." He reached for her.

"I can't, Barry," she said.

He put his arm around her shoulders and pulled her closer to him. "I care very much about you."

Then they kissed.

Belinda pulled away from him, "Does Zelda kiss as

good as I do?"

"I wouldn't know," he said while holding her face between the palms of his hands.

Barry dropped his one hand and cupped her breast over her T-shirt.

Quickly she reached up and took his hand off her breast, shaking her head.

"Belinda..."

"Somebody'll see."

"No, they won't. They're all at that lame game." He lifted the edge of her T-shirt and slowly glided his hand up her waist.

When Belinda opened her mouth to protest, he sealed her lips with a kiss.

In a husky whisper, she murmured, "Somebody's going to see us, Barry."

"Come on, Belinda," he begged.

"I'm not comfortable doing it here."

"I need you so much, Belinda," he said as he unhooked her bra.

They were so oblivious, so lost in their passionate kiss their eyes were closed and perspiration streaked their flushed skin until…

I stood up from the ground and rubbed the dust off my jeans. Then, my hands were pressed against my temples and my throat was filled with silent screams of terror. It looked like a vandal had come along and thrown red paint everywhere. Drops of red goo were dripping from the tips of leaves. Barry's throat was slashed, and Belinda's bloody body laid sprawled across him.

I must have blanked off from shock.

I turned on my heels and ran as fast as I could back to the boarding house and back to my room. Phoning the police was not an option. They would think it was suspicious if I was the first one on the murder scene again.

Instead of asking me a few questions, they would probably arrest me, and I would be locked up in jail. If they asked me questions, I would be unable to answer them, which would make me look even more guilty. All I remember was feeling bad for watching them, feeling rage built up in me until it exploded and then nothing.

9

In the middle of the night, my eyes opened and at the side of my bedroom window, I saw a shadow move but then I turned over to my other side and went back to sleep.

I was walking up a set of stairs, moving down a dark upstairs hallway and into a room. Standing in the centre of the room, I looked at a photo of my dad and Lily on the bedside table, the same photo from the yearbook, only this time my dad had not been cropped out. My eyes looked toward the bed and there was someone sitting right there in the dark.

I backed away until my back was pressed against the cold wall behind me and the shadow on the bed stood, stepping closer to me.

"What are you doing?" I heard my mum's voice.

My dad answered, "I sneaked in. The door was unlocked, so..."

"Fine, but why are you in Lily's room?"

"Guess I wanted to just be here for a minute. I still can't believe she would do that… Walk into the lake like that."

"That's hers?" My mum asked pointing at the Ouija board lying on the bed. "Did you ever play with her?"

"No. I thought maybe I could use it to say sorry..."

My mum sounded shocked. "That's why you're here? You were going to try to talk to Lily?"

"I keep hearing this voice in my head," my dad said. "One and one makes three. What does it mean?"

My mum's eyes stayed focused on the board. "Do you think she's still here?"

"When I came in, I thought I felt something."

"Felt what?"

"I can't explain it. Something."

My mum traded a worried look with my dad. "Do you think she's trying to tell you something?"

"I don't know, Dianne," my dad said with a sigh. "I feel really guilty, though."

There was a creaking noise in the room, and they fell silent, listening.

Suddenly the photo frame of Lily and my dad on the bedside table fell to the floor with a loud shattering noise.

My dad leapt closer to my mum and wrapped her in his arms protectively.

"What was that?" My mum asked with a tremor of fear in her voice.

My dad held his hand up to silence her, he was trying to hear something. He said, "I am sorry, Lily. I never meant for any of this to happen."

My mum pushed him away from her and hissed, "Are you serious, Roger? You never meant to fall in love with me, never meant to have this baby growing in my belly?"

There was no answer.

It was as if even the room was waiting for his reply.

My dad said, "Lily, I know you're here. Tell me what you want me to do."

"She can't be here, she's dead," my mum insisted.

"Then how do you explain this feeling, the photo on the floor?" He pointed to a corner. "There's someone there."

"Where?" My mum squinted in the darkened room trying to see what my dad was pointing at.

"There." My dad kept his finger pointed at the corner as my mum reached for the light switch beside her.

The lamp light flickered on, erasing all the shadows in the room and the corner was empty.

My dad turned to look at me. "I'm worried about you."

The incessant noise of my alarm clock woke me, and I leapt from the bed not even awake yet.

Two hours later, girls dressed for Phys Ed streamed from the locker room. I left the room last, trailing behind because I did not want to listen to them either discussing Shannon's death or the coming Spring break weekend.

It seemed nobody had found Barry and Belinda's bodies yet, but I was starting to think it was all just a crazy dream.

I headed out to the P.E. field and I could feel the weak Spring sun trying to warm my shoulders.

"Alison?"

I turned to see Oliver hiding behind a large shrub to the side and after making sure Mrs Hawkins was preoccupied with the other girls, I slipped off the pathway and approached him. "Why are you here?"

Oliver looked uneasy. "I'm worried about you."

"You could have sent me a text instead of coming here. You're going to get us both in trouble."

"You haven't given me your number yet." He gave me a sheepish grin.

"Give me your phone," I said holding my hand out to him.

He gave me his phone and I added my number to his contact list.

"Have you heard anything else about Shannon," he asked when I handed his phone back to him.

"Nothing. I saw the police here again this morning, so they are investigating it and I'm sure they'll find the killer soon enough."

"I haven't slept since the dance, and I keep thinking there's a psycho killer on the loose."

I chuckled. "Watch a lot of horrors, do you?"

For the first time, it dawned on me that none of the girls were afraid. It was being treated as just a random murder when we are supposed to be protected behind high walls and security gates, a lake at the back of the building and a tiny forest of trees to the side. The setting was so established it was hard to believe someone had been murdered or were able to enter the premises to commit murder. I asked, "You think someone at the dance did it?"

He shrugged his shoulders and admitted, "It had to be

one of us."

"Evan said it couldn't have been a girl, so it must be someone from the boys' school, right?"

"Maybe," he agreed. "It makes me nervous, knowing there's a murderer lurking around." He turned away from me and I could see it was because he was trying to hide his emotions from me.

"Did you really date Shannon?" I asked him. If he did, it must have affected him more than I had realised. "So, you must have liked her, you know... More than friends?"

"We hung out a few times, but I never thought there could be more between us than just friendship. She was always fun to be with."

"We had a minute of silence for her in assembly this morning, you?"

He nodded his head.

"They told us her memorial will be after the Spring break, will you go?" I asked.

"I guess. I wonder if we'll still go camping this weekend and if we don't, what are we expected to do?"

"We could just go home for the break, you know, like normal kids," I suggested.

He shook his head. "Spring break's only a few days long and most of the students here don't go home when the break is so short. After the property was damaged ten years ago by bored students, the school board and the parents' association arranged camping activities or excursions to the city or abroad. Most times, we only go home for the three-week Christmas break and the months of Summer holiday."

I was surprised, but to be honest, it was foreseen that since being abandoned at boarding school I would hardly ever see my mother again. Obviously, she would not see me, at all, but that goes without saying.

"Does everyone go camping this weekend?" I asked.

"Yeah. There's a separate camp for each year group, but boys and girls in the same year group go together, under very strict supervision." He smiled and I saw the crest of his cheeks turn a shade of pink.

"Where are these camps? I hope at least it won't be boring."

"Here at school," he said.

"What? That sounds super boring."

He laughed softly. "Yeah. There are camps around the lake."

"Alison!" Mrs Hawkins' voice shouted from the field.

Oliver said hurriedly, "She's probably thinking you got murdered now."

"I should go. See you this weekend?"

He agreed with a nod. "I came to tell you to be careful. Stay safe."

"I will. You too." I turned away from him and ran back to the field and Mrs Hawkins whose voice was now calling my name in a shrill, panicked scream.

That afternoon, I had a scheduled appointment with Dr Smithers in his office. He wanted to make sure I was not psychologically damaged after finding Shannon's dead body. However, I was sure he did not care about my mental health and it was school policy to evaluate all the students after a traumatic experience.

We sat across from each other for almost ten minutes in total silence as he waited for me to say something, and I was waiting for him to say something.

He was a short man of Asian descent. His eyebrows were large and black, and I was fascinated by the way they almost met in the middle. It was the first time I had ever met someone with a unibrow.

I got a fright when he started talking, "I arrived on Friday night, just as you were leaving the hall and even though I called your name, you continued walking away. However, I noticed you seemed disassociated from the situation and your lack of emotion at this moment indicates the same. I believe you had what we call a psychogenic blackout."

He explained, "A psychogenic blackout can be difficult to diagnose. Most often it occurs in young adults as a result of stress or anxiety."

I nodded my head. If it was so difficult to diagnose, how come he labelled me with it so fast?

He continued, "It is an involuntary reaction of the brain to alleviate distress and sometimes they are a reaction to a horrific experience you have not been able to come to terms with."

Let me count the many ways. I continued to stare at him. Without me even saying a word, he had figured me out.

He asked, "How often are you experiencing these attacks? Do they tend to be numerous, often occurring several times a day, or at the same time each day?"

"I don't know," I said. "Is this serious? Can I die from it?"

He smiled without showing any teeth. "I don't want to diagnose you before we have had a few sessions, but it sounds as if you might have a condition, we call Dissociative Identity Disorder. It is not at all life threatening, but it is likely that there is a temporary problem with the way your brain is working. Your brain may become overloaded with information and shut down for a short while when faced with a threatening feeling, situation, thought or memory."

"What am I supposed to do about it?"

"I'd like your permission to contact your parents and then maybe you and I can meet once a week. Is that okay with you, Alison?"

I sighed and rubbed my palms over my eyes. "I guess."

"Sometimes the first attacks are related to an upsetting or frightening experience, or some other great loss or change and I would like to help you work through these issues."

10

After dinner, Rachel approached me and pulled me gently by the arm into the courtyard to the side of the dining hall.

I glanced around, suddenly feeling isolated with just the two of us, out of view of the other students who were still eating or had gone up to their rooms. "I have homework," I told her. "I should go."

She took a step closer to me. "Alison, what do you think Lily is trying to tell you?"

"Nothing…"

"After you came out of that room, I noticed straight away you were different. You are acting strange and then that message on the cubicle wall next to Shannon…"

"How do you know about that?"

"I know someone who knows someone who works at Constable Fraser's house and you know how people never see the help, so she's overheard some stories…"

"Like what?"

"Like your dad is the one who broke Lily's heart and left her for your rich, snobbish mother."

"So? What's it to you?" Why was this happening to me? How many people knew? Was I now forever linked to the reason why Lily killed herself?

"So," she said sarcastically. "I put two and two together and realised that message on the cubicle wall was for you, and I was wondering what it meant?"

"I really don't know what it means."

"I think you do, though." She smirked as she lifted her forearm and her bangles dangled down to her elbow so that I could clearly see the scars on her wrist. "See. I can relate."

I closed my eyes, feeling a chill.

From across the courtyard, there was a sudden soft sound.

Scratch… Scratch… Scratch…

We both turned in the direction of the sound.

Rachel asked, "Who's there?"

There was no answer, but a breeze ruffled the leaves of a small bush nearby. I peered into the darkness.

Rachel asked in a soft whisper, "Was it the wind?" Then she asked louder, "Who is that?" Rattled she started to back away from me and the darkness toward the door of the entrance hall.

I turned to face her and saw someone standing behind her. Rachel was backing up right toward the figure. "Be careful. Behind you," I warned her.

She swung around quickly.

The figure disappeared and I thought it might have been just a shifting shadow from the way the light was coming through the windows, and the gentle breeze moving through the leaves of the trees.

Even though I knew it could have been no more than shadows, I was unable to shake the feeling we were not alone.

We both jumped when her phone started ringing and she quickly pulled it from her pocket. She said, "Sure. Of course. I'm on my way." She ended her call and looked back at me. "There's something seriously creepy going on here."

I agreed, as I looked up at the building and saw a dark silhouette in the window of room thirteen.

With a resigned sigh, I sat down on a low wall and pulled my phone from my pocket. Scrolling through my contacts, my finger hesitated on my dad's name whose number I would never delete from my phone. I felt a deep, painful loss just looking at his number and knowing I could not phone him. In the past, since he died, I had often felt this way but now the feeling was more intense. I could feel it burning in the pit of my stomach, a feeling so intense I had never experienced the sensation before.

I looked up at room thirteen again, but it was empty now. Just a window which would stay empty and dark forever.

My phone vibrated in my hand and I looked from the window to my screen.

It was a message from Oliver: Are you still safe?

I replied: I think someone's messing with me.

Oliver: Like?

Alison: I keep seeing shadows and things. Sorry! No one else to tell.

Oliver: You can tell me. Anything.

Alison: Do you really think there's a psycho killer running around? Revenge for Lily, maybe?

Oliver: Sometimes.

Alison: Am I just going crazy?

Oliver: NO. I don't think you're crazy.

Alison: Would you believe me if I told you what's happened since I went into room thirteen or would you just make fun of me?

Oliver: I'd believe.

Alison: You could use my texts against me in a court of law!

Oliver: I could, but I wouldn't.

Alison: I think I'll keep my secrets for now. I was just feeling a little freaked earlier.

Oliver: You sure?

Alison: 100%

Was I really the reason why Lily killed herself?

Yes. My dad cheated on her.

Yes. He cheated with my mum.

Yes. My mum got pregnant.

With me.

Then I realised why Lily blamed me. I realised what one plus one equals three meant.

My dad was one.

My mum was one.

Add them together and the sum would be me.

Two people and a baby.

An incredible sense of dread washed over me.

I stood up from the low wall and on autopilot, I walked into the brightly lit entrance hall, turned to my right and walked up the wide staircase to the first floor. When I reached door number thirteen, I stopped and placed my hand on the door handle, turning it at the same time.

I was a little shocked when the door swung open even though I expected it to be locked. Rachel and Sinéad must have forgotten to lock it again when I left it the other night in a sheer panic. If I was so scared the last time I was in this room, why did I come back?

After I closed the door behind me, I found my way across the floor to the bed and sat down on the edge.

I was barely breathing, waiting for something to happen. Nothing happened.

"I don't understand," I said softly. "You wanted me to come here. You wanted my help."

Everything was silent. The room seemed to be somewhere in space where no sound could reach it because I was sure girls were talking in the hallway outside, going to the bathroom, laughing, playful yelling, yet not a sound managed to enter this room.

I curled into a ball on the bed, facing the door, ignoring the smell of years of dust on the bed covering.

I must have fallen asleep, because dreamlike images flashed before me of my mum and Lily sitting on this bed, in this room.

Lily asked, "Is Roger ever going to actually ask me out,

or will he just keep giving me that look whenever he sees me?"

Dianne glanced at Lily. "He will, I'm sure. He's always looking at you with that lost puppy look. Maybe if you made the first move?"

Lily laughed. "Now you're just being silly. Girls don't make the first move."

"Really? This is the year two thousand, haven't you heard you don't have to wait for a boy to ask you to the dance. It's okay to be the one doing the asking."

"My mother would have a stroke if she found out I asked a boy first. Etiquette, my dear." Lily mimicked a snobbish accent.

Dianne shrugged her shoulders. "If you don't ask him, I will."

Lily gasped. "You wouldn't."

"I would."

"You like him too?" Lily looked at Dianne with a shocked expression.

Dianne looked away, unable to meet Lily's penetrating stare.

"Is it true? When were you going to tell me?"

Dianne huffed. "Yes, I like him, but he only looks at you. Besides, John told me Roger is asking you to go with him to the Year-end formal so it doesn't matter if I like him or not, he doesn't even know I exist even when I am always by your side."

"I cannot believe you're doing this to me," Lily exclaimed, standing up to pace.

Dianne looked at Lily with a look of despair. "We cannot choose whom we fall in love with, but you're my friend and as long as you are, Roger will forever be off limits to me."

Lily said loudly, "As long as we are friends, he'll be safe? Meaning if you weren't my friend, he wouldn't even be interested in me?"

Dianne sighed loudly. "That's not what I meant, Lily, and you know it."

"Get out!" Lily shouted.

Dianne looked at her confused. "What?"

Lily screamed, "Get out! Get out! I'd rather have no friends than have friends like you!"

11

I woke up with a start, looking around confused until I realised, I had fallen asleep in room thirteen and I could not even remember coming here. My last memory was sitting in the courtyard, texting Oliver.

From the corner of my eye, something moved and then there was a loud scraping sound of something being dragged across the floor. Quickly I slipped off the bed and reached for the light switch beside the door, just in time to see the bed move away from the wall by itself.

I stopped breathing as my body froze in panic. I felt heavy, paralysed, unable to even twitch a muscle.

Everything was still then as if something in the room was waiting for my next move.

Quickly I reached for the door handle next to me and pulled the door open so fast it banged into my shoulder. My feet slapped against the polished surface of the floor in the hallway as I ran to my room.

It was so late; everyone was sleeping which made my chest feel so tight with fear I could only take shallow breaths. My eyes were darting everywhere. The boarding house was so quiet, room doors were all closed, the fluorescent lights on the ceiling seemed dimmer than usual. If there was a psycho about, now was the time he would get me or, even worse, if it was Lily haunting me… I could feel bubbles of panic push up through my chest.

When I reached my room door, I could not get it open fast enough. I had a feeling something was standing right behind me. After I quickly closed the door, I sat down on my bed and stared at the door, waiting for it to open again.

There was nothing.

Only silence.

Did I imagine everything?

Was I going crazy?

Then my books started hurling themselves off my desk one by one. At first, it was slow and then it became faster and faster, the books travelling across the room at a greater distance. Whatever or whoever was doing this wanted to do me bodily harm.

I convinced myself it was Lily doing this.

She hated me.

My mum always got what she wanted, and it was clear from the dream I had in Lily's room that my mum wanted my dad. When Lily told her they weren't friends anymore, she gave my mum permission.

My laptop slid across the desk and then flew into the wall behind me, missing my head by centimetres.

I jumped up and saw a figure standing in my cupboard, in the shadows. It did not move or speak, there was no face, but it stared at me with a strange reflection where its eyes were supposed to be.

My entire body felt weak with fear and I started screaming until my neighbour, Violet, started banging on my room door, asking, "What's going on?"

I fumbled with the door until it opened, and Violet looked at me with a freaked expression on her face. "What the hell, Alison?"

"I'm sorry," I apologised. "Just an awful nightmare."

She looked at me for a long moment. "Do you need to talk about your dream?"

I shook my head. "I'll be fine." I started closing the door. "Sorry for waking you."

After she left, I sat down on the floor in the corner of my room, pulling my legs up to my chest, keeping my eyes wide open as they swept my room from side to side for any movements.

I did not think I would ever fall asleep again, but I must have. Although it felt more like a memory than a dream.

Red flashing lights started spinning around me and I saw a sheet covered body on a stretcher being loaded into the back of an ambulance.

My dad's voice cried from behind me, "No... No... This isn't happening." Then he walked through me trying to get closer to the ambulance and I staggered backwards, barely breathing, wishing something could make sense.

The red lights swept across me with a creeping menace.

A door slammed closed then – a locker door with notes taped to the front of it, notes with sad messages – and the noise woke me from a deep sleep I did not even know I was having.

I felt too paralysed to shed any tears. I was falling apart, and I was fading further and further into oblivion, no more just invisible to the one, most important person in my life, but invisible to everyone. Was I just imaginary? A fantasy? A dream?

Lily. Did Lily feel invisible too? Fading away as her best friend spoke to her boyfriend, the boy she thought was the one, who promised so many things until he betrayed her and broke her heart, her spirit. After she died, her soul imprinted itself on her surroundings and even though nobody could see her, she saw everything.

Closing my eyes, I took a deep breath, trying to tune out my thoughts, trying to get rid of the feeling that something was wrong with me.

I stood up from my sitting position and stretched my legs which felt stiff after having them pulled up to my chest for so long. The light from my window shifted and I glanced down at the Ouija board still lying on my desk and then the planchette... twisted.

I kept staring at it and then very slowly it started moving across the board by itself. Unable to pull my eyes away from it, the planchette continued its eerie drift across the board from the middle to the engraved word: Hello

Shocked I took a step back from my desk and caught a glimpse of a dark shadow in the mirror on the inside of my cupboard door which for some reason would not stay shut anymore.

The shadow was in the shape of a dark figure and it tilted its head a little to the side when my eyes made contact with the gleam where its eyes were supposed to be.

It was moving closer to me and frantically I searched my room for help, but my room was only filled with shadows.

Tears ran down my cheeks as I stood there frozen in fear. A feeling of hopelessness filled me as the dark figure glided across the floor toward me.

There was a noise like water gurgling down a plug hole, as it whispered, "Lily. It's time to come back."

My eyes widened. I started running toward the door. I had to get out of this room and there was nothing that could stop me.

As I ran down the hallway, I kept looking over my shoulder at my room door which I had left open, until I literally ran into Sinéad. We almost fell over from the impact, but she steadied us and kept us from sprawling to the ground.

"Are you okay, Alison? It looks like you've seen a ghost!"

Only then did I notice all the traffic in the hallway. Girls were running in and out of the bathroom, chatting as they walked in groups to get to class.

Sinéad and Amber walked me back to my room and when I slowly took the first step into my room everything looked normal. There was not a sign of the horror I left behind only moments earlier. I dared a glance at my cupboard and the door was closed.

"We'll wait for you while you get ready for school," Sinéad suggested.

Grateful I nodded my head and quickly got ready for class. Together we walked to the school building where I saw Oliver sitting on the kerb outside the entrance. I walked closer to him while Sinéad and Amber stepped past me, saying, "Bye, we'll see you later, Alison."

I greeted him, "Hey, Oliver."

He frowned. "We were texting and then you just stopped replying. I was worried."

I pulled my phone from my pocket and saw I had more than twenty notifications. "I'm sorry. My head is all over the place."

"You're okay, that's all that matters."

I sighed long and deep. "I feel like I'm in a nightmare I can't escape."

He looked at me concerned. "So, I'll see you this weekend at the camp-site?"

"Yeah. There's no way I'll be staying in my room while there's no-one around."

"Creepy, is it?"

I laughed softly. "Very." I started backing away from him. "I'm gonna be late."

The school bell rang, and he turned away. "I better get going too. I'll see you later?"

The trees to the side of the school building cast long shadows, but I side-stepped them not wanting the darkness to touch me.

12

The yellow school bus stopped in a large, level area on the other side of the lake.

When I stepped off the bus, I looked across the flat, calm surface of the lake and saw the school building on the other side, a darker shade of grey than the surrounding clouds. I was mesmerized by the image.

"Alison?"

I turned around to his voice. "Hey, Oliver."

"Scary, isn't it?" He asked as he came to stand next to me.

"What's scary?" I forced a soft laugh.

"The school from all the way over here."

I looked back at the building in the distance. "Yeah. At least it's far from here. I'm looking forward to this break, that's for sure."

The weak sun shone high above the surrounding trees as the other girls from my year group disembarked the bus. Behind that, the boys leapt with raucous pushing and shoving from a navy and white bus. Not long after, bags were scattered on the ground and the two buses pulled away from the campsite.

Mrs Scott's voice boomed, sending birds scattering from the treetops. "Girls get your bags and move them to the pod you were allocated to yesterday. If you weren't paying attention, wait by the picnic tables until I get to you."

I turned away from Oliver. "Better get going."

"See you later," he said as he walked away to find his own bag and to get settled in his allocated pod.

The pods were built close together and the campsite could accommodate thirty-six students, six per pod and then the four staff members each had their own pod. The toilet and shower facilities were immediately adjacent to the pods and were shared. There was a strict schedule with boy/girl time slots stuck to the door of each pod.

Evelyn called me over. "I've saved you a bed. Top or bottom?"

I looked at the bunk bed. "Bottom?"

"Perfect!" She clapped her hands together with glee. "I was hoping you'd say that."

Glancing around the area uncertain, I wondered if we were supposed to unpack our belongings or what.

Evelyn explained, "I forgot it's your first year. You just live out your bag while we're here. We usually just push them under the beds to keep them out of the way."

I unzipped my bag and pulled a jumper from the top, before zipping it closed again and sliding it under the bed with my foot.

After Evelyn pushed her bag under the bed, she suggested, "We're allowed to keep ourselves entertained until lunch, so Colin, Oliver and I usually go for a walk, are you coming with?"

"Okay," I agreed. This was my first time here and by the sound of it, Evelyn had been coming here every year, so until I got my bearings, I decided to stay close to her.

As we left the pod, Evelyn explained, "Each year group has their own camp-site, so every year it's a different area to explore, so it's quite exciting."

Colin and Oliver were waiting for us and as soon as we reached them Colin took Evelyn's hand in his.

Awkwardly I fell in step next to Oliver and was barely aware of the conversation between Colin, Evelyn and him.

My eyes kept glancing to Oliver, but he seemed oblivious of me as he let his fingers drift over the knee-high grass we were walking through.

My mind started drifting as we came to a clump of trees. A faint mistiness seeped between the trees while the sunlight made long streaks from above the treetops to the ground below. Taking deep breaths, I let the crisp air clear out everything that had happened to me since the thirteenth of February when I walked into Lily's room for the first time. Quickly, I pushed Lily from my mind. The surroundings were too beautiful to let her spoil it for me.

"Are you ignoring me?" he asked.

"It's so pretty here," I said without looking at him and noticed Evelyn and Colin were further ahead.

"There's something we need to talk about."

I stared into his perfect blue eyes. "I don't really want to talk about anything that's happened the last couple of days," I said. "I just want to forget and pretend."

Pretend we met at the dance and you liked me, pretend we never saw Shannon disembowelled, pretend we could be together, be normal.

Oliver shook his head. "No. About you and I."

"Okay?"

"That night at the dance, when we met..."

Birds fluttered from the tree branches around us and I jumped with fright.

Mrs Scott's voice echoed toward us, "Girls! Boys! Lunch!"

Oliver rolled his eyes. "After lunch, okay?"

I nodded my head.

"I mean it. Right after lunch," he insisted and the look in his eyes was serious. He really had the most incredible eyes.

All the way back to the campsite I wondered what he wanted to tell me.

The dining hall had a long serving counter on the back wall and two long wooden tables were set on either side of the large room, from the front to the back, with long benches on each side of them. We queued at the serving counter after grabbing a paper plate from a stack and getting plastic eating utensils wrapped in a white serviette.

Lunch was burgers and chips, and after we were served, Oliver and I followed Evelyn and Colin to a table. The room was filled with loud laughter and happy voices.

Mrs Scott came to stand at the end of our table and waited for us all to look up at her, so she had our full attention. "After lunch, everyone seated at this table will go sailing on the lake. Make sure you take something warm." Without waiting for a response, she turned and walked to the other table.

Oliver nudged me. "Lucky us, we picked the right table. The other table will only get to go tomorrow."

His smile was endearing, and when he looked at me it felt like he actually saw me. A feeling of overwhelming warmth filled me and all I could do was nod.

After lunch, we boarded the cutter with a single mast and a mainsail, one by one. Oliver got on ahead of me and then offered me his hand. I did not need his help, but I wanted to feel his warm fingers curl around mine.

There were benches along the side of the hull, so we sat down as the skipper stood in front of us and gave us safety instructions, the most important one being: When we hear him yell, 'Duck,' we had to crouch down immediately without hesitation otherwise we might get knocked into the cold waters of the lake and never be found again.

I thought he was being overly dramatic about the never being found part, but he seemed serious as his eyes moved from one person to the other until he made eye contact with each one of us.

We pulled away from the dock and then we glided out to the middle of the lake. The breeze got stronger the further we got from the shore.

I leaned over the edge, dangling my fingers in the icy cold water as the boat skimmed along the small waves. It was quiet, except for the shushing sound of the water and every so often the ring of the metal grommet banging against the mast.

A strange feeling came over me as my fingers glided through the water. Its coldness welcomed me. The dark depths felt like home.

A few hairs had come undone from my ponytail and blew in a crazy random way around my face. Brushing some flyaway hair from my face, I asked Oliver who was seated beside me, "What did you want to tell me?"

"Maybe later."

I shrugged. Earlier it seemed so urgent to say what he wanted to say, but I did not want him to think it bothered me that he did not want to tell me anymore.

The wind changed direction suddenly and we crouched down immediately when the skipper's voice yelled, "Duck," as the sail swung around.

"If you could sail anywhere?" He asked me.

I laughed softly. "Don't know. This is my first-time sailing. You?"

"The Bermuda Triangle," he said seriously.

I looked at him and laughed. "That sounds very ominous."

He laughed with me. "Would you miss me?"

"Maybe," I said, looking away.

We sailed around the lake until the sun began to sink toward the grey monolith of the school building.

As soon as the cutter came to a stop next to the dock, everyone jumped down on to it. The supports squeaked loudly under the weight.

Oliver had already jumped off, but something made me wait and I let everyone go ahead of me. For some reason, I liked the way the boat swayed on the water beneath my feet, it made me feel relaxed, it gave me a sense of belonging.

Everyone else walked along the dock back to the campsite, discussing the sailboat, the way the boarding house looked so ominous from this side of the lake, and things I could not make out.

When I did not have a choice anymore, I jumped from the cutter and joined Oliver where he was waiting for me on the dock.

He said, "You know what we should do?"

"What?"

"Hang out?"

"It's almost dark."

"So?" he asked like he had expected me to agree immediately.

"So, I need a shower before dinner." I stared at the ground.

"Okay." There was a note of disappointment in his voice.

I looked up at him. "Afterwards?"

Although I fell in love with his pixilated smile the first time, I saw him, I knew deep down he was going to break my heart.

13

Oliver gave me a funny look. A needy look. He reached out and brushed the flyaway hair back from my face, barely skimming my cheek. My stomach clamped down in nerves as he leaned closer. Then, softly, his lips were on mine.

I felt confused. Two different emotions rushed through me at the same time. A murderous rage and a feeling of overwhelming desire to be happy.

Slowly I pulled away from him and looked at him, brushing my fingertips lightly across his lower lip and then wove his fingers through mine.

Something was happening to me.

We were standing in shadows and the voices of the other kids and teachers seemed distant but I could see their dark bodies etched clearly against the big bonfire they had built on the large stretch of sand between the camp-site and the edge of the lake.

"We should get back," I said.

His shoulder brushed mine as he leaned closer and whispered in my ear, "You don't have to go."

I did not want to go.

He sat down on the edge of the dock, letting his legs dangle over the side and pulled me down to sit beside him. The dock was high enough so that our feet did not touch the cold, dark water. A slight breeze swirled around us making me feel a little cold.

I turned around to face Oliver. "So, are you ever..."

He raised his eyes to meet mine.

Was he looking at… Me?

"Going to kiss me again?" He asked softly as the one side of his mouth pulled up in an amused smile.

Flustered, I said, "No. That's not what I was going to say."

He chuckled softly as he nudged me playfully. "I know. What did you want to know?"

"I… I forgot what I was going to say." I looked down at the water below us and the way the glow from the bonfire reflected off the peak of the ripples the breeze was creating. My legs swung backwards and forwards.

He shook his head. "Remember when I said earlier today, we needed to talk."

I shrugged my shoulders without looking back at him, pretending to be mesmerized by the water.

"It's really dark out here," he said as he looked over his shoulder at the tall, dark trees behind us.

"It makes it easier to see the stars," I said, looking up at the sky.

Oliver lay back on the dock. "There are so many," he said.

"That's because there's no moon."

He laughed softly. "The moon is still there; we just can't see it."

I am like the moon.

I eased myself down next to him and we both watched the sky in silence.

"You know," he said quietly. "I'm glad I kissed you. At first, I thought I shouldn't have done it. It was too soon and I'm not even sure if..."

Then why? Why would he kiss me if he was not sure he wanted to? Did he think he would get his way with me easily? Did he imagine we would go all the way, here in the dark, just the two of us? I know I am not the first girl he had kissed, with whom he had been alone in the dark.

Will I even be the last?

"If what?" I asked softly.

He lifted his head off the dock and leaned on his elbow, then tilted his head toward me and leaned closer, kissing me softly on the lips. He pulled away, and then moved his mouth to my cheek, nose, eyes, brow, his kisses followed a trail determined by him.

I could barely breathe.

He stopped, his face hovering an inch above mine.

I could not read his expression and I was not sure if it was because there was hardly any light or if he was trying to hide his emotions.

I opened my mouth to say something sarcastic to hide the way I was feeling.

"What if?" He asked before he kissed me. His hands

rested on the waist band of my jeans and he looped his fingers through the belt loop on one side to pull me on to my side to face him.

My hands came up to his chest to push him away.

"What's wrong?" Oliver asked, his lips still so close they brushed mine as he spoke.

"Not too fast," I said.

"As slow as you want," he said as his warm hand slid under the hem of my T-shirt.

My top crept up, exposing my stomach to the night chill.

He traced his finger along my waist while kissing the side of my neck. Of course, I had imagined being kissed like this, but the reality was so much more intense.

As Oliver slid his hand higher up my waist, I put my hand on top of his, not sure if I wanted to never move again or if I wanted to make him stop. I was conflicted. My body wanted him to continue, to see where this would lead. The voice in my head warned me he was only using me. He would break my heart. If I let him continue, he would discard me like a used rag.

"Too fast?" He asked and he sounded concerned.

"I think so, yes," I said softly.

Slowly he pulled his hand out from under mine and making small, lazy circles on my skin which gave me goose bumps he moved his hand slowly down my waist until his hand was resting on the waist band of my jeans again.

14

I put my head down, hiding my face to avoid his eyes.

"Hey, guys," Evelyn said. "We were looking all over for the two of you."

Looking up, I saw her and Colin, silhouetted against the night sky, their shapes hovering above us.

Quickly I moved away from Oliver and sat up, folding my arms around my legs as I pulled them up to my chest.

"Can we join you?" Colin asked as he sat down next to Oliver, dangling his legs from the dock.

I lifted myself quickly. "I need to go to the pod for a second."

Evelyn glanced in my direction. "Hope it's not something I did."

Colin agreed, "Just as we arrive, you run off."

I chuckled dismissively. "I need the loo if that's okay with the two of you."

"Have you been here since we got back from sailing?" Colin gave Oliver a bemused look.

As I walked away from them, I heard him say, "Yeah. I wanted to talk to Alison, but we got side-tracked, a little."

Evelyn giggled and each note from the sound escaping her mouth cut like a piece of glass through my soul. She had turned the moment, which a second ago felt special, into something dirty.

They were laughing at me.

I won't allow Oliver to hurt me.

No-one will ever hurt me again.

The forest loomed dark beside me and from the corner of my eye I saw a shadow move across the tree trunks to my side and then there was a flash of silver, maybe a reflection off an old discarded can. The wind whistled through the branches above my head and it sounded like a whisper, "Alllliiisson."

I spun around, peering into the dark, trying to see if there was something between the trees.

My heart started pounding in my chest. "Is someone there?"

A voice said softly, "It's me, Lily."

I was not sure if the voice came from the darkness between the trees or if it came from inside my head.

Terror threatened to overwhelm me, and I took a step back before I twirled around and bolted as fast as I could to the campfire and the safety of light, not looking back.

Mrs Scott called my name as I sprinted past her, but I did not stop.

I was running away from me and I could not run fast enough.

I only slowed down when I entered the communal bathroom, leaning against the cool, beige tiles to catch my breath. The small light bulb overhead barely lit the two white porcelain basins against the opposite walls from the puke green stall doors, which were pushed shut and had pockets of shadows hiding behind them.

Pushing away from the wall, I walked to the first stall slowly and pushed against the door to push it open before walking in. Silhouetted in the shadow, behind the separating wall of the neighbouring stall there were two feet in the bottom gap, I gasped as I took a step back.

When I looked again, the pink Vans were gone and then a hand grabbed my wrist making me stumble in panic.

"Alison?" The girl asked.

I yanked my hand down hard to release the hold of icy cold fingers around my wrist and looked down, glimpsing a long sharp blade.

I hardly managed to turn before the long steely blade rose high in the air. It came down with force and I felt a warm oozing liquid splatter my face as the knife thrust in and out of the girl's chest who tried to put up a fight but it was useless, she never had a chance. Then she fell to the ground with a limp puppet motion.

In terror, I took a couple of steps backwards and slipped down the smooth tiles on the wall behind me until I was sitting on the cold concrete floor. I felt numb and scared to death as I stared at the lifeless body and then I heard a voice screaming and screaming, not realising the sound came from me.

Oliver came running into the bathroom and ran straight to me, pulling me up from the floor and the screaming stopped.

He was going to think I had committed all these crimes. He was going to think I was the psycho killer on the loose. The girl he kissed was the mass murderer. I had to get away from him. I would never be able to handle the loathing in his eyes. I would become invisible to him as well.

Shoving him away from me, I pushed past the gathered crowd to get out of the room.

Wiping my hands over my face, I felt the sticky sensation of the blood now glued to my skin and panic again threatened to overwhelm me.

I had to get away from here.

Aiming for the trees, I sprinted across the open clearing as fast as I could.

I could hear Oliver's voice calling my name and his footsteps were pounding the ground behind me.

His voice became further and further away as I ran in between the trees. My foot got stuck in a fallen branch and I fell on to the ground. I squirmed until I got up on my hands and knees, looking over my shoulder in the direction I came and saw nothing. Only darkness.

Then I heard voices right beside me, on the other side of a large bush.

The girl was crying softly. Quiet, whimpering sounds.

The boy's voice said, "It just happened, Carly. I love her. I never meant to fall in love with her, but it just happened. I am sorry to do this to you."

Rage filled me and a red hazy mist started swirling

between the trunks of the trees surrounding me. It seeped up from the ground and curled its wispy tendrils around the branches.

Then the girl was screaming, and I saw a bloodied body on the ground next to her. He was gutted from the neck down and his insides had become his outsides.

Turning, I saw Oliver racing toward me. "Alison, we have to get out of here," he screamed. "There's a killer running loose."

I kicked my legs in front of me to scoot backwards. "Don't come any closer, Oliver," I warned him.

The bright glare of a flashlight blinded me for a second and two people, one on either side of me started to lift me from the ground.

"This camping trip is over," Mrs Scott said to the side of me. "The entire camp is a crime scene and we all have to get back to the dorm as quickly as possible." She was standing a few feet away from me, her expression was dismayed.

I was terrified. Could I trust these people?

The way the flashlights threw dancing shadows on their faces made them all look like pure evil demons. The shadows made their mouths look full of little sharp teeth, and their eye sockets were bare. When I was on my feet again, I took a step away from them.

Mrs Scott was trying to calm everyone and telling us, "Follow me. We need to get out of here." In a tightly formed group, they started to rush back toward the campsite.

Taking a couple of steps backwards into the dark forest, I collided with Oliver who had moved to stand behind me.

I spun around to face him.

He grabbed hold of my hand and I saw a frown flicker across his face. Lifting my hand, he looked down.

When he looked back at me, his face was etched with shock. "Alison? Where did you get this knife?"

I looked at my hand which he was holding up between us. Clutched between my fingers there was a long, silver knife covered in blood.

A knife I never realised I was holding.

My fingers felt numb and lifeless. My knuckles were a strange yellowish colour.

I pushed him hard against his chest, knocking him onto his back. I straddled his chest and my fingers grasped tighter around the knife in my hand as I lifted it high above my head and I stabbed him, again and again.

"Alison?" His voice croaked as a pinkish foam frothed from between his lips.

Drawing small circles on his chest as my finger glided through his blood, I replied, "Alison hasn't been here since the night she met me."

THE END

For more stories by

STEPHEN SIMPSON

visit

www.stephensimpsonbooks.com

Continue reading a short bonus flash fiction story…

MY ENTRY INTO THE ABYSS

I have what they call a tick. My head moves involuntarily from left to right, left to right continuously. Sometimes I can control this movement of my head, this constant denial to everything around me, but not for long.

Dr. Anderson is supposed to cure me, and he says every day we make progress, but let me tell you right from the start, that he is talking utter nonsense.

I am on my way to see him now; my head starts ticking more than usual. I have a deep settled fear in the pit of my stomach as we walk down long passage after long institutional passage, whilst my head moves in sync with my feet. Left, right, left. I know there is something wrong, there must be a reason why I am afraid every day when the white, round clock tick, ticks its way too fast to two o'clock.

I stop in front of the brown laminated door with the

dull bronze letters, spelling out DR. ANDERSON and then the trouble starts. My head starts to shake so violently that spit spews from between my lips. My feet cannot step over the threshold. Fear pushes up from my stomach into my chest, past my lungs and into my throat. I can feel the fear sitting there with the mash potatoes I had for lunch.

The two burly attendants on either side of me lift me by cupping my elbows in their big hands and they carry me across the room towards the brown sofa along the wall, squeezed in between the grey metal filing cabinet and the window with the twelve-inch black bars welded into the concrete.

Dr. Anderson with his kind smile rushes towards me and gives me my daily fix. Amen.

I feel the familiar prick of the needle and then the warm flood of 'mooty' spreads slowly, but surely through my body.

Dr Anderson smiles down at me, after the attendants let me drop onto the sofa. He says kindly, "All better now, Agnes?"

I smile up at him. My lips say, "Yes." My head moves from left to right, left to right.

He turns away from me and sits down in the chair across from me. The chair he sits in every day.

He says, "Okay, Agnes. You know how it works. Lie down, fold your hands across your chest and close your eyes."

I lie down onto the brown sofa. It is soft and I can feel

it sink in under my body. I fold my arms across my chest, I cross my legs and I close my eyes.

"No, Agnes. Uncross your legs. Every day I have to tell you the same thing."

I uncross my legs.

He sighs. "Okay. Take a deep, deep breath."

I take a deep, deep breath. I feel my chest rise.

He says, "You are in a big, white circular room."

I look around and see that I am in a big circular room.

"There is only white, brilliant white all around you"

I look around me. There is only white, brilliant white around me.

"You look up and you cannot see the roof. Everything is white."

I look up. Everything is white and I cannot see the roof. The room is so huge.

"You look down and the floor is white."

I look down. The floor is white.

"You see across from you, a dark brown door."

I look ahead and there is a dark, brown door.

"You walk towards this door."

I start to walk towards the door.

"You see a large silver door handle."

I look at the large silver door handle.

"You reach for the large silver handle and you push it down."

I fold my fingers around the large silver handle, and I push it down.

"You open the door slowly."

Slowly I push the door open.

"You see before you the most beautiful peaceful scene, you have ever seen."

I see a big, black, dark pit.

"You see a sky so blue and clear. The grass is bottle green and neatly mowed. You hear birds singing and you hear the faint gurgling of a river."

I see and hear nothing.

"You step onto the green, green grass."

I step onto the stair leading the way deeper into the dark pit.

Read the beginning of Chain Letter

LONG AGO

Sparks, like bright orange fireflies spiral into the sinister darkness of the night sky, as if funnelled up by an unseen hand from the huge fire in the centre of the imposing mud huts build around it.

The ridges of the mountain surrounding these huts are darkly silhouetted against the black heavens. The heavy drumming and moaning of many voices echo up into the sky and then outwards into the night.

There are no other sounds, no night birds, no crickets, no frogs - they have all hushed their nightly serenades on this night where the moon hangs colossal, round and white in the sky, floating just above the horizon.

The thunderous, continuous rhythm of the drumming stops abruptly as if gulped down by an unnoticed mouth.

A woman walks into the circle. She is tall, pale, and beautiful. The moon reflects off her ebony black hair hanging down to her waist. As she lifts her long elegant arms up into the air, she screams a blood-curdling scream.

Her face distorts as she screams, turning her once beautiful features into a nightmarish, misshapen façade. Her eyes are deep and black, and reflected within them are the deepest recesses of torment and misery.

She wears a loincloth made from the skin of a leopard around her hips. Her naked breasts sway with her every movement. Around her neck hangs a necklace of leopard's teeth, tightly strung together, representing protection.

Every living being in that circle, around that fire, falls immediately, their bodies flat against the ground. You can taste the fear, thick as peanut butter stuck to your palette.

The fire reflects and dances a frenzied dance in her eyes, making them sparkle with malevolence. She smiles in anticipation for what she knows is coming. Shivering and gyrating, foam coming from her mouth, her eyes roll backwards in their sockets and she starts to mumble the same incoherent string of words repeatedly.

Six men walk into the circle carrying a wooden board. Their faces are turned downward, their expression and facial features hidden. The glow from the fire shimmers off their brown bodies, glistening with oil.

On the wooden board lays a girl of fifteen. She is dressed in nothing. Her hair is plait with the feathers of many coloured birds. Her face is painted with the warm blood of chickens. She is terrified and frightened.

Her moaning is now the only sound in this hushed space, surrounded by the imposing mud huts. She knows her fate and she has seen many girls go before her, the monthly ritual that feeds their god, a god with an unquenchable thirst for human blood. Her ankles and wrists are dripping with blood from where she fought against the ropes that bind her.

The six men walk towards the pale woman and then lay the girl down in front of her, before falling to the floor, their bodies spread close to the ground.

The inhabitants of this village have served her, their god, all their lives, and so did their fathers before them and their fathers before them. They have not seen her grow a day older, so they believe that she is immortal, above them and they fear her with every thread in their bodies, a fear inherited down from generations upon generations of ancestors. She has a skin so pale, as none of them has ever seen before. Her hair is long, as theirs would never be and then the fact that she is never-ending, everlasting makes them believe, beyond a doubt that she is indeed their god. She is not a forgiving, loving god, but a cruel and evil god. She leads through fear, pain, and suffering.

The woman stops chanting. Sudden silence fills the air, except for the crunch and crackle of the fire and the soft moaning of the girl lying before her on the ground.

She takes out a knife from the folds of the loincloth wrapped around her lower body and then she holds it up into the night sky.

The light from the full moon catches the blade and it glistens brightly.

The woman screams again—long, loud and piercing. Her eyes roll backward into their sockets as she swiftly bends her knees and plunge the knife into the girl's heart.

The young girl looks up into the sky, focused on a star where she believes her soul will ascend to. She listens to her own scream mingled together with the scream of her god. It echoes away over the mountains into forever.

The light in her eyes is fading fast. She senses a darkness soaring towards her, she feels herself moving towards that distant star.

Then she can feel the pressure of her god draped over her chest. She can hear her god drinking greedily, swallowing fast the blood pumping, and draining from the wound where the knife is extracted.

1

Marlene sits down at her desk and tapping the escape button on her keyboard she brings her computer to life.

With the soft humming of the computer surrounding her, she looks over the screen out the window at the clear blue sky. She has never seen this exact colour of sky before, the blue is almost an aquamarine, but then again it is more of a sea blue, or maybe it is more of a turquoise.

From the corner of her eye, she notices that the computer is ready for her, all her personal settings initialized.

Absent-mindedly she folds her hand over the mouse, moving the white arrow across the screen. She double-clicks the button to open the Internet icon.

Immediately the screen opens and then she waits patiently while the computer waits for the page to load – website found, waiting for reply.

She thinks frustrated that it is time to upgrade to a faster computer. She spends most of her day waiting and she feels as if she is forever waiting for pages to open, waiting for documents to print, waiting, waiting, and always waiting.

How much time is wasted waiting? Yes, she now saves time by not standing in long queues at the bank, because she can do all her banking on-line. She saves time not waiting at the checkout, because now she can buy everything her heart desires off the Internet, with only a knock on the door announcing that it has arrived. All her friends now are avatars.

She really uses the Internet mainly as a giant public library, searching for information on travel, hobbies, places of interest and general information. She also does some emailing to keep in contact with her family.

Although they say that the Internet is also an entertainment dome, playing virtual chess and other games against unknown challengers, she has never attempted this. She has also never downloaded music, a television program, a movie, or a book, preferring the old-fashioned method.

Only once, did she enter a chat room, but felt inadequate. They all spoke so fast, in as few letters as possible and still to this day, she does not know what they were trying to say. She felt ousted and nobody bothered chatting with her anyway. Just imagine, a world where she could be unpopular although no one knew whom she was, what she looked like or her real name. She logged off, embarrassed. Chat rooms are mainly for the young - under twenty-five-year-old - in her opinion.

The Internet has been around only for a few years now and they say that people are already losing contact with their physical social environment, using the telephone less;

it is easier to send a mail. People are reading fewer newspapers, watching less television, and spending longer and longer hours surfing the net, thus spending less time in shopping stores and commuting in traffic to and from shops.

Marlene works Monday to Friday at a job she loathes with a passion. She wakes up with aches and pains, tired and in real need of more sleep. She often wonders how funny it is that on a weekend she awakes fresh, invigorated, able to take on the world, but come Monday, the world rests heavily on her shoulders.

Eventually the page opens in front of her and she double-clicks on the link that will take her to her email provider. She enters her username, her password and then reaching with her pinkie she pushes the enter button.

Once again, she waits while the page loads. Normally she would open another page while she waits for one page, but today she does not feel like multi-tasking and besides, it only slows down her computer, bought only last year, but already seriously outdated.

Her mailbox opens and she has seventeen unread messages. She notices most of these are from companies, companies she orders from, or that she once had a query about and completed her email address into the field provided and now, she is on their mailing list, a valued customer.

There are only two emails she will bother opening, the one from her daughter, Lisa, and then the one from her daughter-in-law, Adèle.

Lisa now lives in England with her husband and Marlene's two grandchildren, Paul and E'lisa. Lisa only wrote a few cursory lines, as usual.

Lisa says they are well, the weather is awful and that she is frightfully busy. Marlene considers amused that Lisa almost sounds as pompous as only the English can. Lisa continues, promising that she will attach photos the next time she mails. Marlene has heard this many times before and never has she seen the icon indicating that a mail from Lisa has an attachment.

Sighing Marlene moves the email to the folder named Lisa; she will reply tomorrow.

She selects all the mails from the companies she has no intention of reading and moves them to her trash folder.

Double-clicking on Adèle's email, Marlene notices too late the three letters FWD in the subject-field. Softly she swears under her breath. She hates these emails with a passion; emails that need to be forwarded or you will encounter doom. Admittedly she does not forward them all and none of the doom prophecies has come true, such as if you delete this mail, your left foot will rot, start to stink and fall off within one week. Low-and-behold she still has both her feet.

BOOKS BY STEPHEN

Chain Letter
Murder Gone Viral
The Invisible Girl in Room Thirteen
What My Soul Does When I Am Asleep

The Girl in Room Thirteen & Other Scary Stories

Triple Six series
666 Mark of the Beast
666 Pestilence

Zombie Girl series
UnDead Girl

Stephen Simpson writes scary stories with gasp endings. He is the bestselling author of The Invisible Girl in Room Thirteen, and the author of horror fiction. He has always had a vivid imagination, and now uses this to inspire the stories he tells. A full-time author, Stephen lives in Northern Ireland with his family.